THE DEVIL'S
MOTOR

First published circa 1911
This edition published in 2017
by Suffolk & Watt, London

A CIP record for this book is available from the British Library
ISBN: 978-0-9932999-4-0 (paperback)
ISBN: 978-0-9932999-5-7 (ebook)

THE DEVIL'S MOTOR

MOTOR

— A FANTASY—

MARIE CORELLI

FOREWORD

The English novelist Mary Mackay (1855 —1924), was known by her pseudonym, Marie Corelli. She was a literary success from the publication of her first novel, *A Romance of Two Worlds* in 1886. She faced criticism, however, from the literary elite of the day who derided her work as "the favourite of the common multitude".

The success of the novels was due in part to a public increasingly fascinated with spiritualism. A recurring theme in Corelli's books is her attempt to reconcile Christianity with reincarnation, astral projection, and other such mystical ideas. She was apparently associated with the Rosicrucian organization, Fraternitas Rosae Crucis.

For over forty years, Corelli lived with her companion, Bertha Vyver, to whom she left everything when she died. She did not identify herself as a lesbian, but several biographers and critics have noted the importance of her erotic descriptions of female beauty in her work.

Corelli, however, was known to have expressed a passion for the artist Arthur Severn, who was the son of Joseph Severn and a close friend to John Ruskin. In 1910, she and Severn collaborated on the dark fantasy, *The Devil's Motor*, in which Severn provided the illustrations. In the story, the motor car is depicted as a vehicle of evil — symbolic of the destructive forces of greed and modern industry.

Corelli warns that we must not let the speed of progress make us *"forget to halt to gather the flowers of thought… the fruits of feeling."*

Bizarrely the original publication of the book, with its specially commissioned binding, was made to smell like petrol. Unfortunately, whatever was used to create the smell was highly acidic, causing the pages to disintegrat over time making copies rather rare today.

This edition reproduces the text of this intriguing book without the illustrations or the smell.

THE DEVIL'S MOTOR

— A FANTASY —

In their dead midnight, at that supreme moment when the Hours that are past slip away from the grasp of the Hours yet to be, there came rushing between Earth and Heaven the sound of giant wheels, — the glare of great lights, — the stench and the muffled roar of a huge Car, tearing at full speed along the pale line dividing the Darkness from the Dawn.

And he who stood within the Car, steering it straight onward, was clothed in black and crowned with fire; large bat-like wings flared out on either side of him in woven webs of smoke and flame, and his face was white as bleached bone. Like glowing embers his eyes burned in their cavernous sockets, shedding terrific glances through the star-strewn space, — and on his thin lips, there was a frozen shadow of a smile more cruel than hate, — more deadly than despair.

"On!" he cried — "Still on! On with an endless rush and roar! Over the plains of the world that is gone, — over the heights of the world to come — on. still on! Without pause, without pity, without love, without regret! Follow me, all ye Forces which are destined to work the ruin of Mankind, — follow! On. on, over all beauty, all tenderness, all truth I ride, — I, the avenger, the Destroyer, the Torturer of Souls, the Arch-enemy of God! The Kingdom of Hell grows wide and deep, — praise be to Man who makes it! I count up my growing possessions in the ever breeding spawn of human lust and avarice, — I breathe and live rejoice in the poison-vapours of human Selfishness! The men of these latter days are my food and sustenance, — the women my choice morsels, my dainty delicates! Brute beasts and blind, they snatch at every lie I offer them; — rejecting Eternal Death, — verily they shall have their reward! Like a blight my Spirit shall encompass them, and whosoever would scour the air and scorch the earth must run on the straight road of his desire with Me!"

The great Car flashed along grinding, thunderous wheels, and as it flew, vast Phantom-forms followed it, like rolling clouds jagged with the lightning,

— the fairness of the world grew back, and sulphurous flames quenched all sweetness from the air.

The forests dropped like broken reeds, — the mountains crumbled into pits and quarries, the seas and rivers, the lakes and waterfalls dried up into black and muddy waters, and all the land was bereft of beauty. In the place of wholesome green fields and leafy woods, there rose up gigantic cities, built-in on every side, and bristling with thousands upon thousands of chimneys belching forth sickening smoke into the overhanging gloom which hid the skies; and the cities were full of a deafening noise and crashing confusion as of ten million hammers beating incessantly — beating away all peace, all solitude, all health, all rest.

On, — on, and into these countless prisons of stone and mortar the Demon of the Car swept vast and every-hurrying crowds of human beings, with the furious force of a mighty whirlwind sweeping dead leaves into the sea.

"No room to breathe — no time to think — no good to serve!" he cried — "Now shall you forget that God exists! Now shall you all have your own wild way, for Your way is My way! Now shall you resolve yourselves back to an embryo of worms and apes, and none shall rescue you, no, not one! For the Seven Angels of Judgment Day are sounding their trumpets of terror, and who shall silence their Voices, or stay the thunderings and lightnings, or the great earthquake?

Hail and fire! — and the trees, and the green grass burnt up and destroyed! — the sun and the moon, the day and the night smitten into one blackness! We will have no more virtues! — no more hopes of Heaven! Honour shall be as a rag on a fool's back, and Gold shall be the pulse of Life! Gold, gold, gold! Fight for it, stealing! — pile it up, hoard it, count it, hug it, eat it, sleep with it, die with it! Lo, I give it to you in millions, packed down and pressed together in full and overflowing measure — I scatter it among you even as a destroying rain!

Build with it, buy with it, gamble with it, sell your souls and bodies for it, — there are devils enough in Hell to drive all your bargains! Sneer at truth, defeat justice, snatch virtue's mask to cover vice, drug conscience, feed and fatten yourselves with the lusts of animalism till the cancer of sin makes of you a putrefaction and an open sore in the sight of the sun! Come, learn from me such wisdom as shall compass your own destruction! Unto you shall be unlocked the under-mysteries of Nature, and the secrets of the upper air, — you shall bend the lightning to your service, and the lightning shall slay! — you shall hollow out the ground and delve a swift road through if for yourselves in fancied proud security, and the earth shall crumble in upon you as a grave, and the cities you have built shall crush you in their falling! — you shall seek to bind the winds, and sail the skies, and Death shall wait for you in the clouds, and exult in your downfall! Come, tie your pigmy chariots to the sun, and so be drawn into its flank vortex of perdition! All Creation shall rejoice to be cleansed from the pollution of your presence, for God hath sworn to give unto Me all who reject Him, and the Hour of the Gift has come!"

Still faster flew the Car,– red meteors flashed in its course — and the Phantom shapes which followed its flight crowded together in an ever-thickening, ever-darkening multitude, while bright stars were shaken down from heaven like snowflakes whirling in a winter blast. And, mingling with the grinding roar of the wheels came other sounds, — sounds of fierce laughter and load cursing, — yells and shrieks and groans of torture, — the screams of the suffering, the sobs of the dying, — and as the Fiend drove on with swift quickening fury, men women and little children were trampled down one upon another and killed in their thousands, and the Car was splashed thick with human blood. And He who was clothed in black and crowned with fire, shouted exultingly as He dashed along massacred heaps dead nations and broken remnants of thrones.

"Progress and speed!" he cried — "Rush on, world, with me! — rush on! There is but one End– hasten we to reach it! No halt by the way to gather the flowers of thought, — the fruits of feeling — no pause for a lifting of the eyes to the wide firmament, where millions of spheres, more beautiful than this which men make wretched, sail on their courses like fair ships bound for God's golden harbours1 No time to listen to the singing of the birds of hope, the ripple of the sweet waters of refreshment, the murmur of cool grasses waving in the fields of peace; — no time, no stop, — no lull for quiet breathing, — on! — forever on!"

Up and ride with me all yo who would reach the goal! Come, ye blown and bursting windbags of world's conceit and vain pretension! Come, ye greedy maws of gluttony — ye human pottles of drink, — ye wolves of vice! Come, ye shameless women of losts and lies and vanities! Come, false hearts and treacherous tongues and painted faces! — come, dear demons all and ride with me! Come, ye pretenders to holiness — ye thieves of virtue, who give 'charity' to the poor with the right hand, and cheat your neighbour with the left! Come, ye gamblers with a Nation's honour, stake your last throw! Come, all ye morphia-fed vampires and slaves to poison! — Grasp at my wheels and cling! On-on-over the fragments mighty Empires, — over the hearts of kings and queens, — over the lives of the brave, the good and the wise! — trample them all down and crush them into dust and ashes! What shall we do with wisdom, we who have done with God? What with purity? — what with courage? Naught are these but reproach and bitterness — mere obstacles in the roadway which leadeth to destruction; — ride them down! On-on! To the destined end! — on with rush and hurry and panting eagerness to reach the only goal — the last of winning posts — the close of Certainties, — the GRAVE!"

Like a flashing blur of fiery wheels the Car now spun along in the blackness of the night, and the drifting Phantoms round about it were as great grey sails swelling with the angry blast, and sweeping it onward through the dark.

"Pray no more — hope no more — love no more!" cried the Fiend. "Be as the shifting sands, or as the trembling quicksilver — inconstant, capricious — ever in motion, never at rest! Change — change and revolt! All ye who weary of old things, behold I give you new! Bodies shall be pampered and souls killed for your pleasure; — foulest vices shall be called merely 'sensations', — each to be tried, excused and condemned in turn, — and virtues all have no more place at all in the scale of feeling! The music of life shall clash into wild discord — the love home shall be lost glory, — tenderness for the young, and reverence for the old, shall be faded sentiments of the past, only fit for the mummer's jest! Change — change and sensation! Roll out your columns of vaporous notoriety, ye printing-presses of the world! — spread wide the fame of the Anarchist and the Courtesan, — mock and revile the spirits of the wise and true, — noise abroad the name of the Murderer, and treat the Poet with derision — give flattery to the rich and scorn to the humble, — teach nothing but the art of lying, — and venom to the tongue of scandal, — dig up the graves of the great, and kill the reputations of the brave and pure!"

Help nothing on that is noble, — nothing that is honest, — nothing that is of God, or for God, — print every lie, grudge every truth, and let your trumpet-note be that of blatant Atheism and Devilry the the end! Set trade against trade, — community against community, — nation against nation, — until with your windy bombast and senseless twaddle you fill your witches' cauldron of mischief and contention to the full! Up and ride with me, ye Plotters against Peace! — ye whose hands are against every man! — there is time to be lost — up and away with a rush and a roar! — for the Great Star has fallen from Heaven to Earth, and to Him is given the key of the bottomless pit! The pit is open — the gate stands wide — up, and speed on with Me!"

Like lightning now the great Car tore through space — its flaring lamps flashing, its wheels grinding with the sullen noise of a bursting volcano, — and amidst cries and shrieks indescribable, it leaped, as it were, from peak to peak of toppling clouds that towered above and around it like mighty mountains. And presently it seemed as if a thin, pale line of purple fire glimmered afar off, and by this light was seen a monstrous ridge of dense blackness jutting sharply over some vast incalculable depth of horror: On — still on — the Car rushed; and He of the sable robes and flaming crown urged apace its reckless speed with wild shouts of wilder laughter.

"All the word in such haste to die!" he cried. 'All the world gone mad with the craze of movement! Up in the air, down on the earth — all turned to whirling, flying, tossing atoms of dust in a storm and lo, the End! Be patient now, for ye shall never wander again! — be silent now, for prayer and cursing laughter and teas are done! — let the hoarded gold drop from your grasp — it can purchase nothing yonder! Was it worthwhile think you, — this rush headlong, to be cast into silence?"

Was it worth while to leave the sunshine for this dark? — beauty for this decay? — sweet sounds of love and tenderness for this still glow of the eternal flame which is not quenched — this gnawing of the eternal worm whose appetite is never satisfied? Lo, ye have burnt up a world to light Hell with its flame! — but the world shall blossom again like a flower springing from dust and ye whose soulless lives have been a curse and an outrage on its fairness, shall pace its pleasant paths no more!

Rejoice, O earth! — rejoice, O sea! — to be freed of the burden of Mankind! Rejoice, O birds, that the hand of the spoiler shall no longer wound or slay! — rejoice, O trees, that the axe of the destroyer shall no more cast ye down! — rejoice, O all ye living creatures of the filed and forest, that Treachery no longer stalks the world in man's disguise! Take back the planet, O great God, cleansed of a pigmy race! Create a new Humanity! — for this is past!"

On — on, — along the black ridge jutting darkly over silent Immensity, with a whirl of fire and roar of thunder the Car flew, — and then — as if for one brief breathing part of a second it paused!

Like a vast Shadow between Earth and Heaven the Demon stood — his body hand on the steering-wheel — and every point in his flaming crown scintillating with the sparkle of a million stars.

Roound about him soared and stooped countless terrific Phantom-shapes — some like wrecked ships — some like torn flags of honour — some like mounted warriors — some like throned kings — some like fair women veiled in a mist of tears, — and beneath his bat-like pinions, outstretched to north and south, there glimmered a pale crowd of white faces, upturned wild eyes and imploring hands — all crushed together in a writhing mass of agony! But no sound came from those dumb mouths agape with terror, — all were silent as Death itself, and only the thunderous roar of the Car echoed through space, as after that; infinitely brief pause, it dashed furiously onward and down! — down, — down sheer over the edge of that mystic precipice into the fathomless abyss of the Unseen and Unknown!

A thousand lightning leaped after it — a thousand crashing echoes vibrated through the Universe with its fall, — one frightful human cry shuddered up to heaven, — and then — silence.

Gradually, gently, and by faint degrees, a glimmer of pale gold divided the darkness with the wavering rise of dawn — a cool wind parted the air into sweet breaths of fragrance — and in the centre of the awful

stillness a scaled sun rose slowly, fixing the red seal
of God on the closed history of the world!

OTHER GREAT TITLES FROM
SUFFOLK & WATT

Available online and in all good bookshops

*   *   *

The Adventures of Thomas Pellow
Three and twenty years in captivity among the Moors
by Thomas Pellow

**Drawing Attention
to the Israeli-Palestinian Conflict**
Political Cartoons by Carlos Latuff

Story of a Country Town
by Edgar Watson Howe